Donut

The Unicorn Who Wants to Fly

Story by Laura Gehl ♥ Art by Andrea Zuill

RANDOM HOUSE STUDIO ⌂ NEW YORK

Donut jumps!

Donut thumps.

Donut jumps!

Donut flumps.

Donut slumps.

Donut sails!

Donut flails.

Donut wails.

Donut dreams.

Donut schemes.

Donut beams!

Donut tries.

Donut ties.

Donut flies!